Lee Aucoin, *Creative Director*
Jamey Acosta, *Senior Editor*
Heidi Fiedler, *Editor*
Produced and designed by
Denise Ryan & Associates
Illustration © Holli Conger
Rachelle Cracchiolo, *Publisher*

Teacher Created Materials

5301 Oceanus Drive
Huntington Beach, CA 92649-1030
http://www.tcmpub.com
Paperback: ISBN: 978-1-4333-5483-0
Library Binding: ISBN: 978-1-4807-1139-6
© 2014 Teacher Created Materials

My Life as a Bee

Written by Sharon Callen

Illustrated by Holli Conger

Baby Photos

I was a beautiful baby.

3

I have bright stripes and strong wings.

4

stripes

strong
wings

5

Flying Lessons

This is my first flying lesson with Dad—I crashed.

This is my second flying lesson with Dad.

I crashed—again.

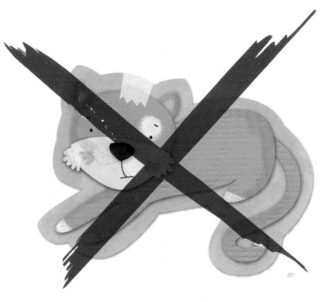

This is when I crashed into a nasty cat.

Worst, Worst Day

This is when the nasty cat chased me.
You wouldn't believe how fast he was!

More Flying Lessons

This is my third flying lesson, when Grandpa taught me how to fly.

Look
at me!

15

Best Day

When I could fly faster,
I chased that nasty cat.

Best, Best Day

This is when Grandpa gave me his goggles.

All Grown Up

Now, I am
a busy bee!